Lacrimosa:

a Tragic Love Story in Three Acts

Faith May Griffin

Wider Perspectives Publishing ¤ 2023 ¤ Hampton Roads, Va.

Lacrimosa:

A Tragic Love Story in III Acts

a Poetry Collection by

Faith May Griffin

© 2023, Faith Griffin,
1st run complete in October 2023
Wider Perspectives Publishing, Hampton Roads, Va.
ISBN 978-1-952773-77-8

This is for you.

Prologue: Wreck

He was a lighthouse
when she met him,
tall, solid, built to endure.
He had weathered many storms
but had never succumbed
to the damage.
His eyes were a beacon
drawing her towards him.
He warned her
that if she came too close
she would wreck
and it would be the end of her,
but she didn't listen,
and it was.

Contents

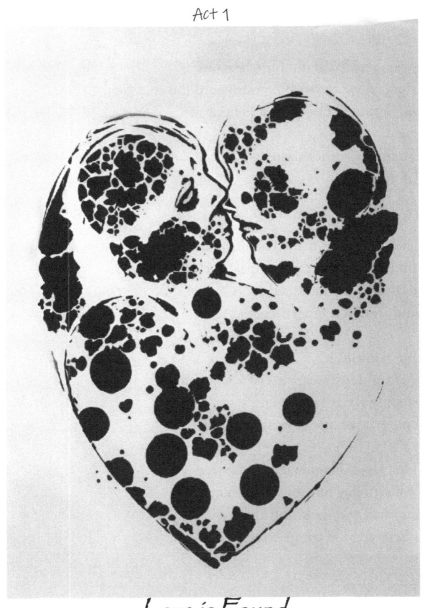

Love is Found

Pizza Parlor Love Story

Your eyes like lighthouse beacons
shine high above tilting cardboard towers,
not even the fluorescent lighting
can find flaw
on that beautiful shoreline
of your jaw.

Only teenagers
and those who made bad life choices
find themselves pushing past each other here
in this sweat thickened shop,
and I was a repeat offender.

But you and I,
we could be the misfits of the misfits,
sharing clever pizza puns
and greasy hash browns at midnight.

June kisses illuminated by the tree
still standing in your living room
adorned with gold and glass,
discussing the complexities
of sadness
and poetry.

Lacrimosa:

Your hands cover mine completely,
and your skin smells of smoke.
Driving home, my ears still echo
with your ab-aching laughter.

My body begs for more
streetlight meetings,
bruised knees from your passenger seat,
dark mischief in your eyes
when you pause for water,
mouth dry,
but nothing else.

Greedy for more
of your passion and prose,
I find myself craving
some hot Dominos.

Tresspassing Together

Trespassing together
hand in hand
dressed to match the darkness,
sneaking under the fence
with our dollar store flashlights
laughing as they flicker,
turning quickly when
we hear creepy sounds.

We're only here to see the stars
in their natural habitat
but the sky is too cloudy tonight,
not a single fire to be seen
or even a glimpse of the moon.
We lay on our backs
in the grass anyway
and I contemplate in silence,
next to his electric body
how much like a chocolate
easter bunny I am,
carved with a smile on the outside
but snap off the head by the ears
and there's nothing inside.

He breaks the quiet
with a swift point of his finger
"Lightning bugs." he says.
"You mean fireflies?" I ask,
"Nobody calls them that," he says.

"Well I'm going to call them
starbugs." I tell him.
"Like the coffee shop?" he asks.

I open my mouth
and exhale
every ounce of breath
to make room,
then slowly but with hurricane force I inhale,
pulling in and capturing
every single starbug in a 5-mile radius,
and shut my mouth.

They spread through my arms and legs.
my fingers and toes
until I'm glowing like the sun.
He turns to look at me
bursting with laughter
at my puffed-out cheeks
and the ridiculous look on my face.

Gently, so as not to hurt them
I open my mouth and let them fly out.
I am empty once more.
No, not empty
this space is reserved
for him.

Love Poems

My heart-
the inkwell for my pen
once overflowing like a fountain

a Bellagio of ballads
that could fill 1,000 feather quills

that could write
enough songs and sonnets
to fill the continents with
my calligraphy
the valleys with my verses
the sands with my scripts

once deep enough
to hide sunken ships
filled with gold and secrets
begging to be uncovered

once vast and immeasurable
like the beautiful darkness
above our skies

Lacrimosa:

once innocent and beating
in perfect iambic pentameter-

My heart-
the inkwell for my pen
once tipped over and wasted

a loss of blood and spirit
the seeped through the cracks in the floor

once dried up liked a desert
with remains of refrains
scattered and lost
once left to die
with retreating boot prints
as permanent features

My heart and my pen
once stopped writing poetry-

then I met you
and the fountain flowed once more.

Day Moon

Sometimes the moon
catches a glimpse of you
at night
and lingers
well into the day
in the hopes of
seeing you again.

The Beginning

Until I met you
I had never met a man
with as many smiles
as I own dresses
and I don't know why
I continue to be
surprised
at how often you
surprise me
but you're not like other men
and I own many dresses.

When the right corner
of your mouth
lifts into a sly smile
followed quickly
by your right eyebrow,
I know that my cheeks
are about to flush red
from the filthy words
ready to fall from your lips.

When we're riding in the car
and you look over and see
that I've been looking at you too
an adorably quick smile

Lacrimosa:

unfailingly pops up,
faithfully followed by
an adorably quick kiss.

Often your smile turns in on itself
hiding your lips completely
while your eyes get twice as wide
when I've done something embarrassing
and you're trying
to hold back
the laughter that will soon explode.

I don't mind when you
beat me at Uno
or scare the shit out of me
for the hundredth time
by simply hiding
around the corner
because your playful smile
is more beautiful
than a plastic bag dancing in the wind.

My favorite smile
is the one
when both sides lift at the same time
as your eyebrows and your eyes
say I love you
before your mouth does.

Sometimes you smile
when you're angry
and although I know
it's because you
don't want to upset me,
I know
that smile.

If only I could
remember to water the plants
I could grow you
a garden of patience,
violet in color,
that would give that smile
serenity and new meaning.

I have seen the smile
you paint on
when you're feeling pain,
it's your eyes that give you away.
They look as if they're searching
for the light
that once flickered inside them.

If only it were as easy
as sharing the flame
on the tips of sparklers
we could both light up the night.

Lacrimosa:

If only my body were a window
you could pull up the blinds
on my chest
and see that my heart
beats in time to your footsteps
and my blood flows along rivers
that follow
the sound of your voice.

You could peek
through the curtains
into my mind
and watch my dreams as I sleep
and see that my thoughts
and visions are all
versions of you.

If only you could see
through the panes of my body,
to look inside me and know
that what I tell you is
true.

You hear me talk about love
but these are not love
poems.
I have loved and been loved before
and that's not what this is.

Love
can be replicated.
Even the love a parent
has for their child
gets repeated with each
new addition.

But this.
This cosmic interference
in our otherwise mundane
human life cycle has elevated us
to the level of gods
in each other's eyes,

This is not love,
it cannot be copied or
cloned and I don't have
a word to define it
or describe it
because it did not exist
until I saw that first
smile.

That first smile
that held the universe inside
like a kaleidoscope
of prismatic prophecies.

You could see our story
from start
to never-ending
if you only knew
where to place your eye.
No one else has ever seen
that smile
since it was sculpted
just for me
in the only medium
more stunning
than Greek marble.

When you gifted me
that first smile
my vision blurred
behind these frames
and when I removed
my glasses, my eyes
worked perfectly
for that one, single, moment

and I could see
not only distance
but the future.

Your smile was the end of the past
and the beginning
of us.

Hold On

I don't even need to close my eyes
to feel the back of your neck
in the palm of my hand
holding you close to my chest

Your arms engulf me completely
like the heat
on a sweaty summer day
But when I walk alone at night
You seem as far away as the stars
Even though I see you in every shadow

This feeling of loss when I'm not with you
is not one of a puzzle missing a piece
it is a feeling of missing your entire skin
every inch of my body feels it

And like a balloon in the hand of a child
I have nothing holding me here
when you are not here
holding me.

You

You're sitting on the floor
in front of the mirror
smudging your black eyeliner
while David Bowie sings
about a space oddity.

You're thinking about that man
who makes you feel
like a puppy
broken free from his leash
tongue out and wild
with joyous abandon.

How did you get
so lucky?
The way he cradles
your fingers so gently
when he brings them
to his lips
and sends a morse code
of kisses
across the surface
of your skin.
What is he saying?

Lacrimosa:

Why you?
What's so great about you?
What could he possibly
love about you?

And then
you hear
the ticking
of the clock
out of nowhere
even though
it's always been there.

And now
you can't
stop hearing it.
It's so loud
so obvious
why
didn't
you notice
it
before?

What else
have you
ignored?

Obsessive thoughts
is what
she wrote
on your chart
and now
you can't
stop thinking
about it.

Every tick
of the clock
is a pound
you can't lose
a joke
that wasn't
funny
a stumble
a bad angle
smeared
lipstick
food
in your teeth

embarrassment
shame
guilt.

Obsessive thoughts
they turn
and tick
around
and around
like the hands
they don't stop
debt
doubt
P
T
S
D

Ground
control
to major
tom
your
circuit's dead
there's
something
wrong, wrong, wrong, wrong.

Cover your ears
close your eyes
hold your breath
fold up tight
listen
for something else.

Can't you hear it?
Open your eyes.

You're not
on the floor anymore
you're in a hammock
under a tin roof
swaying
in a summer's rain

Listen
it's not ticking
you hear anymore
it's sprinkling
it's splashing
it's raindrops
tap dancing
it's the sound
of sins
washing away

Lacrimosa:

it's the melody of
redemption,
forgiveness.

It's the sound
of your laughter
mixed with his
that brings you back
every time.

Home

She hated her name
it didn't feel like home.
She wanted to be one
with him,
never alone.
She changed her name
to his,
so that no one
could tell them apart.

Those Moments

I am happiest in those moments
when my name crosses your lips,
when your hand reaches for mine
not out of habit
but out of desire for my touch.

I am happiest in those moments
when we're laughing so hard
that we're breathlessly begging each other to stop
but we can't
cause you've snorted and sent me off
rolling around on the floor.

I am happiest in those moments
when you've fallen asleep
wrapped around my body
your slow, calm breath on the top of my head
bringing a breeze of comfort to my hair
and my thoughts.

I am happiest in those moments
when you apologize
for saying I love you
too many times in one night
but this isn't just one night
and you could never say I love you
too many times in one life.

Lacrimosa:

Mittens

I tore my bed frame apart,
dragged it to the side of the road
and now my mattress
sits on the floor.

The bedposts had
been standing over me
like pallbearers
as if I was sleeping
in a coffin
which is what
it feels like
when you're not beside me.

Sometimes when
I look at you
it's as if I'm
seeing you for the
first time
like Brad Pitt
looking around
the garden
with his vampire eyes
and I want to tell you
that you complete me,
but that's just not enough

Lacrimosa:

since I was nothing
until I met you
and you can't
complete a person
that doesn't exist.

On a night when
I couldn't warm
your hands with mine
I made you mittens,
oatmeal in color
like a sweet warm breakfast
on a chilly morning.

Each stitch representing
one thing I love about you
and there were hundreds
of stitches
sorted into rows.

One for your smiles
one for your impressions
one for the colors
your eyes become
depending on your mood.
One row for your
ticklish spots and
one row for your
collectibles.

The thumb on the right
is made up of all
the ways you cuddle our cats,
the thumb on the left
is surprises you've
brought me when
I'm not even sad.
One row is for
the ways you love
your family
and one row is for
the ways you love me.

The last three rows
are made up
of individual traits
and experiences
that make you
uniquely you.

When you hold my
hands in these
handmade mittens
it means I'm
in the middle
of a moment
that will one day
be a memory.

Lacrimosa:

And maybe one day
I'll make us a quilt
stitched with those memories
that will warm us
on a mattress
that sits on the floor.
We'll watch vampire
movies and gaze at
each other as if it was
the first time we met
and fell in love.

Let Go

He will make
an amazing father,
but she cannot
give him a child.
They should just
end it now,
but neither one
can let go.

Lacrimosa:

Our Love

Some people say
that love
is like a roller coaster
full of rolling hills
curves and loops
highs and lows
but not our love.

The thing about roller coasters
is that there are safety features
checks and buckles
brakes and rules.

You can see the track
and know what to expect
before you even get in line.
It's a relatively safe, and short ride.
but not our love.

No, our love is more like
a rusty 60's style ski lift
soaring above the gaping
mouth of Mt. Vesuvius.

At any moment one of us
could plummet into the
waiting pool of fire
and the other
would jump in headfirst
to bring the other back.

Some relationships
are like butter
melting across the warm surface
of freshly baked biscuits
they meld together and become
impossible to separate
or even identify
the extent to which
one has taken over the other.
But not our relationship.

No, our relationship is more like
Bertie Bott's every flavored bean
we may look impossibly similar
on the outside
but bite down
and you'll find out just how different
we are on the inside.
Now, I'm not saying
one of us is vomit

while the other is kiwi
but I'm saying
that you can't truly
appreciate one extreme
without the other.

Love can be like a flowing river
lazy in some parts
rapid in others
there will be dams
that slow life down
and waterfalls that speed it up
but a shared destination
will keep this kind of love
on a predetermined path.
But
not our love.

No, our love is more like the readout
of an ekg machine
sharp, severe peaks
and dropoffs that go straight down
but we always come back
and keep moving forward
those zeniths and chasms
are the indicators of life
not
the smoothness in between.

Lacrimosa:

Mornings

I love you most in the mornings
When we haven't had a chance
To ruin each other's day yet

Love is Lost

The Fog

A fog has settled
inside our house,
at times it's so thick
that I can't see you clearly
even when you're
standing right in
front of me

I reach out for your hand
but find only shadows instead
this heavy, gray intruder
has seeped into every corner,
has found every crack
in our foundation
and I don't know
how to make it dissipate

Someone let it in
or maybe we both
kept the door open
too long without
realizing we were
being followed
but either way
it won't go away
on its own

When I scream at it
you think I'm screaming at you,
and when you try to ignore it
I think you no longer notice me,
this fog has come between us
and it's blocking the sun

It snuck in so slowly
I can't pinpoint
exactly when it showed up
and sometimes it feels like
it's always been here,
sitting so comfortably in our house
like it was an invited guest

I don't want to leave
I don't want to stay
I just want to see you again
I want to feel your breath
in my ear
your palm on my cheek
your lips on my lips

Maybe if
you close your eyes
and I close mine
I can call out your name
and you can
follow my voice,
we don't need
to wait for a clear day
to find each other again.

Lacrimosa:

Crowded

At night I snuggle up
against your body
turned away from me

In the morning
you accuse me
of hogging the bed

Alone

She can feel him
on her skin
surrounding her,
even when they are apart,
except when they've been fighting,
then she can't feel him
at all.

A Sinking Ship

I saw it from miles away
the sun shining off its hull
the waves holding it up
like an offering from the gods

The boat wasn't brand new
it had scratches and splinters
but it was beautiful and unique
I climbed on board
maybe too quickly
but I was drawn to it

I could see our future together
adventures and voyages
the wind blowing through my hair
flowing
like your sail

We left the world behind us
without a second thought or glance
the smile, permanent on my face
while I slept
splayed out across your deck

Lacrimosa:

Even when I felt the water
licking my bare feet
I just smiled
and looked up to your highest point
feeling your body surrounding me
with promises of safety

The skies weren't always clear
but we made it through every storm
your strength
carried us both

The sunset was brilliant pink
when I felt the water up to my ankles
but I just skipped across you
laughing and splashing

I stacked wooden pallets under my bed
to lift it
out of the salty puddles
and went back to cloud watching
and daydreaming

We saw dolphins and whales
perform their private dances
and fish leapt to my fingertips
as I leaned over the side of your railings
pretending
my knees were enjoying their bath

When I woke up one morning
and my nose was the only thing
still above the waterline
I was forced to take a look around me

My beautiful boat was sinking

It had been sinking this entire time
but my eyes had refused to focus
instead, they had been drifting,
blurred by the lure of a life
not meant for me

I grabbed a bucket as it floated by
and desperately began
sending the water back into the sea
as if I could single handedly save you
as if I could single handedly save us
as if it wasn't far too late
as if I hadn't done this to myself
again.

I tried so hard to keep us together
I threw everything out
my bed, my dishes, my books
my passions, my individuality
my self-worth

I don't need anything but you
how can I live without you
I'm stranded in this ocean
and you're the only thing
keeping me from drowning
I need you
don't leave me

My tears are just filling you up faster
I'm making you leave faster
I can't even feel you under my feet
anymore

You're gone

My head is somehow still above water
my body suspended near the surface
kept afloat with my own meager movements

How long will I drift here, alone?
how long until
another beautiful boat sails by
and pulls me in?

I Used to Love the Rain

I used to love the rain,
and then I met
a storm cloud.

I didn't know that's what he was at first-
When I met him
he was calm and gentle,
but by nature
a storm cloud is shifty
and unpredictable.

A sunny day
turns into a gentle mist
turns into a dreary drizzle
turns into a heavy downpour
turns into
a vicious torrent.

The lightning
that would crash down,
when he was the darkest of grays,
was swift,
piercing
and seemingly unprovoked.

How does one forecast or prepare-
for the kind of
anger-charged electrical current
that only nature understands?

The only way to stay safe
was to make myself small
and try to hide
until he passed.

A storm doesn't last forever
and soon the sun would begin to peek through,
the rain would dry up
and forgiveness
would settle in.

It's easy to fall back in love with the rain
when the clouds are bright
and the breeze is warm,
and it's easy to forget
about the threat of darkness
when you force yourself
to pretend
that you're not scared.

But over time
the dry spells between storms
grew shorter instead of longer
and the shadow above my head
seemed to settle in for good.

The hope of sunny days
turned into the hope of drying quickly
turned into the hope of treading water
turned into the hope of
surviving the storm.
The scars on my skin
were not from him,
a cloud has no hands
with which to cut.

But the scars on the inside
were raised by his terror,
fear was his instrument,
and the thunder
was
deafening.

Lacrimosa:

Glass Bowl

I was the glass bowl
you cupped in your hands
filling me with oatmeal
to warm you
on chilly mornings
washing me with care
and bubbles.

Holding me once more
for a game among friends
strips of paper I offered
with suggestions of gestures
laughing and passing me
from hand to hand
I was the center of your world
for moments out of days
and that was enough for me.

Then one day you
just
let go
I fell to the floor
shattered and fleeing
you were frightened
of what I would do to you

Hurrying to throw me away
every single piece of me,
I was broken
and you just tossed me
in the trash
with the bones and plastic spoons
reminders of what had once
been in your mouth

Like the edge of mine,
when you drank that
last sip of soup
and I tasted your lips
right before you
carelessly let me slip.

Hourglass

Hand in hand we stood
shadowed by the monumental
hourglass that was our love.
We watched for a moment
as the granules of sand
slowly poured into the lower chamber
like the hissing of a snake.
As the beaches and deserts of the world
loomed above us
the echoes of our laughter
leapfrogged higher and higher
until they disappeared like a wispy cloud,
never to reach the top
of the seemingly infinite
gold and glass vessel.

When silence took over,
our voices run dry,
our pockets spilling over with stolen sand,
we turned and headed home.

We spent our love like lottery winnings,
heavy handed and reckless
sprinkling trails behind us as we ran,
building sandcastles that touched the sky,

Lacrimosa:

burying the floors of our home six inches deep,
just so we could leave footprints
for each other to follow.

We measured our love in buckets and pails,
dug holes with shovels
so we could bury each other
up to our necks,
and when the breeze blew
the sand into our picnic lunch,
we laughed and toasted
to our sandy-wiches,
and to the imaginary camels
who trudged across the dunes
that had once been
our grass covered lawn.

But one morning,
I woke with red eyes
and scratched irises,
knowing it was finally time to wash the sheets.
Later,
I noticed you had cleaned the kitchen,
complaining that you were tired of chewing gravel.
At some point the grass has grown back,
our soles cold on the barren floors,
and the buckets had been lost in the back of a closet .

One chilly night,
I laid my head on your chest
but your arms did not wrap around me
as they had every night since the beginning.
Your hands ran as far away from my body
as they could,
a crucifixion instead of a cocoon.

In the morning I walked
With lonely palms
to our towering time keeper.
The sun shone blindingly
through clear empty glass.
The last grain had fallen
and there was no love left to give.

I beat my hands against the sheer walls
until fractures appeared
across the surface of my heart.

Cradling my splintered fingers
I had a thought,
maybe if we could get the sand
from the bottom
back to the top again
we could start over.
We could be gentle and patient with our love,

Lacrimosa:

we could savor it, keep it safe
and share it in quiet moments,
we could start over and make it last our lifetime.

I ran home carrying hope with both arms
like an overinflated beach ball,
ready to toss it into your waiting embrace.

But when I got home
The driveway was empty,
the front door wide open
and the air was stale,
as if no one had ever lived there
at all.

Bare Minimum

My sanity and ability to love
followed him like the pied piper
when he left.

They danced behind him
spinning in the moonlight
never looking back,

Now I am the bare minimum
of bones and electrical impulses.

I write his phone number
in the margins of self help books
so that people like me
will call him
and remind him of me,

and maybe one day he'll call me
and I can tell him I'm sorry
and the phone
won't dissolve in my hand

like last time
when I heard his voice
telling me
the end.

In Fair Verona

My heart
is not broken
that would imply
it could be fixed

Shattered maybe
yet that would mean
it was whole
to begin with

My Heart began with a hole
that only grew deeper
over time
and I couldn't understand
what I was doing wrong

Why I couldn't find my love
my soulmate, my Romeo?
Years passed before I finally realized
I never would find my dark hair poet

Not because he didn't exist
but because I wasn't Juliet
in this tragic love story

I was nothing but a name —
the minor role,
if you could even call it that,
of Rosaline

My character doesn't require
an actor
it doesn't need screen credits
I don't have any lines
because I don't have any say.

I am an idea, a place holder,
a filler, a practice run,
the opening act
for the main event
and I am all but forgotten
the moment
she steps on stage.

Faith May Griffin

Lacrimosa:

There is No Happy Ending

Scars

I'm waiting on my knees
in the dirt where you left me

My tears fall like the leaves
from the trees that surround me

The sun is going down
but my eyelids resist the temptation

I can still see the shape
of your lightening legs

As you bolted from this place
and from me

I dig a womb shaped hole
in the soil below me

I crawl inside
and begin to think

That you were just a dream
and these scars were self-carved

Maybe if I sleep long enough
I can dream of you again

I close my eyes and invite the worms
to cover my skin.

The End

Out of anger
you've separated your skin
like the front and back cover
of your favorite novel

out of desperation
you're searching for the way out
realizing that this isn't a
choose your own adventure book
because no matter which page you flip to
the outcome is always the same

you've never believed in fate
yet you can't seem to leave
this path
predetermined by your past

choice is nothing but an illusion
and the magician always knows
which card is in your hand

you bind your skin back together
sew it up tight with burnt ligaments
Frankenstein's monster style
because you've always thought
scars were beautiful

Lacrimosa:

since
"stay with me forever"
is your shooting star wish
even though you have a hard time
holding on to
anything

bulk trash pickup
comes every week to your curb
hauling away discarded lamps
and lovers

mountains of meaningless trinkets
pepper the landfill
holding onto your fingerprints
as the only evidence
that they once belonged

When you one day find your place
in that palace of tossed asides
there won't be a single fingerprint left on you
only the hieroglyphics
drawn with fire and blade
serving as your eulogy

wiped clean like a crime scene
your skin bears no memories
of the hands that once held you close

that owned you
that held you down
until you learned to breathe
underwater instead of drown

Not every story has a happy ending
or a lesson learned
and sometimes you just wish
you never picked that book up
in the first place

You thought life would change
with each turn of the page
each chapter an opportunity
for something new
but although the author had a thesaurus
she didn't have a single original thought in her head

everything is exactly as it seems
sometimes the words are just a little
more flowery or the flow is a little more feathery
but the meaning never changes
and neither does the end

Floating

Alone and naked, not afraid
floating in the vast darkness
of this liquid island.
My eyes open to stars above
and to fireflies who dance across the surface.
Deep breath, holding tight
my body lifts high in the water.
My toes and other tall points
feel the wind breezing by.
Exhale and sink down,
surrounded by darkness and warmth,
it touches me all over
with hands that are gentle.
I envy the world of the fish below,
to have the life of scales and fins,
of fluid motion in emotionless suspension.
There is no love, no heartache,
no loss, no regret.
Languidly I float back to shore,
until sharp gray rocks scrape my skin.
I am the drowned man,
the beached whale,
the wonder for tourists to marvel at.
The crabs will march across my chest
picking off little pieces of my flesh,
and the birds will help with the task.

Lacrimosa:

Old Friend

Relapse is the kind of word
that sits quietly in the back of your throat,
like a dark, brown toad
who waits in shadows
to jump out
and scare little girls in fancy dresses.
You can feel it inhale deeply
filling its thin, bulbous lungs with dank oxygen.
It exhales
and you smell the sickening sweetness of vomit,
it reminds you of home.
Addiction rolls around in your mouth
like a ten-cent jawbreaker
from the corner store,
with so many sweet layers
it lingers forever.
The smoky smell of filtered nicotine
winds through your brain
like a spiral staircase,
made of dark metal
with specks of brown rust in the screws
that hold it together.
The taste of liquor with its warm, calm nature,
nurtures and numbs.
A look from across the room,
a knowing, a nod.

It's coming, you can feel it.
You try to swallow it down,
but that old toad won't be stopped.
You used to be one of those little girls
in fancy dresses,
but you didn't run away scared.
You picked that ugly creature up
and gave it a home.

Past Lives

I woke up this morning
and remembered everything,
five births and four deaths
and the lives in between.

In my first life
I dreamt of being a jester.
I wanted to bring joy
to those around me
and hear their laughter.
I painted my face
and danced a funny dance.
It was tears that came
not laughter, though.
Don't be scared,
I would say,
this makeup covers skin
this smile covers lips,
but it made no difference
I was nothing but a fool.

In my second life
I was a cat
sleek and slate gray.
I dreamt of a lap

to sit in
a hand to smooth my fur.
But instead, I found cruelty.

My purring
turned to hissing.
I scratched and ran
from evil hands
and hid and slept
in dampened corners,
voluntarily
discarding the eight other
chances I was gifted.

In my third life
I was a prisoner
isolated, cold
in a cell of darkness.
Forgotten, hungry
and dreamless.
I stopped counting
the days
and started
counting them down
instead.

My fourth life
was the happiest.
I was a child in pink dresses.
I loved dancing,
and I dreamt of worlds
full of candy
and stuffed puppies.

My fourth life
was my happiest
but also the shortest.
I never had the chance
to grow out of those dresses
and it ended before I
knew what to look for
or what to be afraid of.

Now I am in my fifth
and final life.
I know it is my last
because I am nothing new.
I am a combination of
the fool
the cat
the prisoner and
the child.

I scare people off when
I try to make them happy
I run and hide
from the cruelty of others.
I am isolated and forgotten
and I've never recovered
from the death
of my childhood.

Outsider

In the same way that sunshine
can be spelled with yellow,
outsider can be spelled
with blue and gray.

It is a word like trauma or relapse,
words you wish you didn't know how to
properly use in a sentence
describing yourself.

You know what the word outsider
feels like, as if it had been made
into a weighted blanket
that was used
to tuck you in at night
and you can still feel it heavy
on your back throughout the day.

It's not that you're feeling
sorry for the person you are,
it's that you're grieving
for the person you never will be.

For that person that should
have a place to call home
that's safe and warm

and allows you to cry
as freely as you laugh
and always feels like
you belong.

Outsider is a word
that you carry with you
like a birthmark,
some days you forget it's even there
it's been a part of you for so long.

Then there's the days
where it glares so brightly
you have to close the curtains
and bury your head
to try and block the light

It will pierce through the cracks
in between the fingers
of your closed hands
that cover your eyes
as you beg
for a loss of memory.

Night

I used to be terrified of the dark.
When I finally started going out at night
it wasn't because I was no longer
scared of the dark.
It was because I was no longer
scared of dying.

Ghosts

Alone but for ghosts
in each shadowed room
the underbed monsters
the barely there moon

I don't want to be here
and neither did you
but you already left
it's just me now
in this tomb

My teeth chip
when I grind
and shift
while I sleep
my dreams
show me lives
of smiling tortoises
and ladybugs
who speak

One lands on the quilt
pulled up
close to my cheeks
she is someone i knew
but flies off
when I weep

The snow froze
overnight
and the footprints
are clear
a path to my window
the curtains are sheer

I slept with a knife
and a gun
by my side
companions standing watch
while he watched from outside

He left before sunrise
like a restless night's fog
the stars
the foxes
the living have all gone

I slide out of bed
drag my feet
cross the floor
pulled into each room
over thresholds
of missing doors
I rifle through boxes
of fabric and books

Faith May Griffin

Search hidden cupboards
even the ghosts overlooked

Under blankets of dust
and abandoned spider webs
I find what I seek
and crawl back to your bed

A photo of you
before there was color
only gray and its absence
captured and bordered

If he comes back tonight
he will find me
no longer alone
and when the second sun comes
I can finally go home.

I will take you there with me
though your eyes can not see
I hold you close to my ear,
secrets whispered quietly

Alone but not lonely
until both of us fade
then I'll become the ghost
that makes others afraid

Creeping across snow
leaving a path of boot prints
looking for window faces just
to prove I exist

Requiem in D Minor

If life is a journey
then death is our destination
and like Lacrimosa,
Mozart's final piece
mortem interrupts
and leaves even
requiems incomplete
weeping and cursed
on this deathbed.
Aren't we all?

Lacrimosa:

FIN.

colophon

Brought to you by Wider Perspectives Publishing, care of James Wilson, with the mission of advancing the poetry and creative community of Hampton Roads, Virginia.

This page used to have many cute and poetic expressions, but the sheer number of quality artists deserving mention has superseded the need to art. This has become some serious business; please check out how *They art...*

Tabetha Moon House
Travis Hailes- Virgo, thePoet
Nick Marickovich
Grey Hues
Rivers Raye
Madeline Garcia
Chichi Iwuorie
Symay Rhodes
Tanya Cunningham-Jones
      (Scientific Eve)
Terra Leigh
Raymond M. Simmons
Samantha Borders-Shoemaker
Taz Weysweete'
Jade Leonard
Darean Polk
Bobby K.
      (The Poor Man's Poet)
J. Scott Wilson (Teech!)
Gloria Darlene Mann
Neil Spirtas
Jorge Mendez & JT Williams
Sarah Eileen Williams
Shanya – Lady S.
Jason Brown (Drk Mtr)
Ken Sutton

Kailyn Rae Sasso
Crickyt J. Expression
Se'Mon-Michelle Rosser
Lisa M. Kendrick
Cassandra IsFree
Nich (Nicholis Williams)
Samantha Geovjian Clarke
Natalie Morison-Uzzle
Gus Woodward II
Patsy Bickerstaff
Edith Blake
Jack Cassada
Dezz
M. Antoinette Adams
Catherine TL Hodges
Linda Spence-Howard
Martina Champion
... and others to come soon.

the Hampton Roads
      Artistic Collective
      (757 Perspectives) &
The Poet's Domain
are all WPP literary journals in cooperation with Scientific Eve or Live Wire Press

Check for those artists on FaceBook, Instagram, the Virginia Poetry Online channel on YouTube, and other social media.

Hampton Roads Artistic Collective is an extension of WPP which strives to simultaneously support worthy causes in Hampton Roads and the local creative artists.

Made in the USA
Middletown, DE
27 July 2024

58057253R00064